big & SMALL

Original Korean text by Gyeong-hwa Kim
Illustrations by Yeong-seon Jang
Korean edition © Yeowon Media Co., Ltd.

This English edition published by Big & Small in 2014
by arrangement with Yeowon Media Co., Ltd.
English text edited by Joy Cowley
English edition © Big & Small 2014

ISBN: 978-1-921790-58-4

Printed in Korea

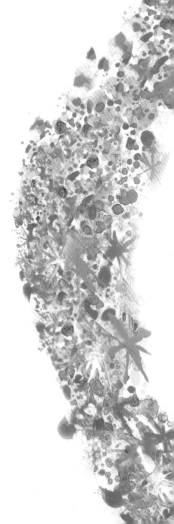

Peter Pan

A story by James Matthew Barrie

retold by Joy Cowley

Illustrated by Yeong-seon Jang

Wendy was telling a story
to her brothers, John and Michael.
Suddenly, a young boy and a fairy
flew through the window.

"Who are you?" asked Wendy.

"I am Peter Pan," said the boy,
"and this is fairy Tinker Bell.
We come from Neverland.
It's an island where children
never grow up."

Peter Pan looked around the room.
"Have you seen my shadow?
I think I dropped it here last night."

"Was that your shadow?" said Wendy.
She took a black shadow from a drawer
and stitched it to Peter Pan's feet.

"Thank you, Wendy," he said,
and he gave her an acorn necklace.

6

Peter Pan liked Wendy. He said,
"Why don't you all come to Neverland?"

"We can't fly," Wendy replied.

"That's not a problem," he said,
"Tinker Bell will help you."

Tinker Bell sprinkled silver dust
on Wendy and Michael and John.
The children floated out the window.
They were really flying!
They were going to Neverland!

As they flew through the air,
they looked down and saw an island.
Neverland was very beautiful,
but what was that noise?
Bang! Bang! Bang!
Someone was shooting at them!

"Be careful," said Peter.
"It's Captain Hook and his pirates.
Tinker Bell, they saw your bright light."

Tinker Bell flew away.
She felt angry and sad.
She thought that Peter
did not like her anymore.

Tinker Bell was so jealous
that she flew very fast
to the children of Neverland.
"Hey!" she yelled, "That flying girl
nearly killed our Peter Pan!"

The children shot arrows at Wendy,
who fell to the ground.

"Stop! Stop!" cried Peter Pan.
"Wendy has come to be our mother!"

"Oh!" said the children. "Tinker Bell lied."

Luckily, Wendy was not dead.
The arrow had hit the acorn necklace
that Peter had given her.

13

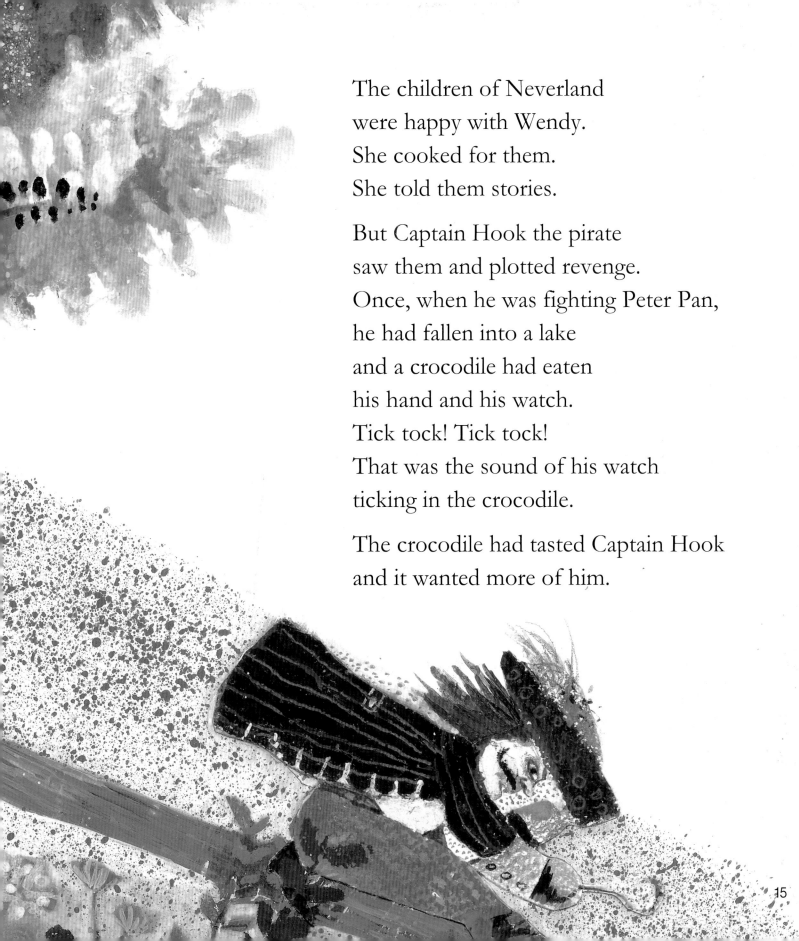

The children of Neverland
were happy with Wendy.
She cooked for them.
She told them stories.

But Captain Hook the pirate
saw them and plotted revenge.
Once, when he was fighting Peter Pan,
he had fallen into a lake
and a crocodile had eaten
his hand and his watch.
Tick tock! Tick tock!
That was the sound of his watch
ticking in the crocodile.

The crocodile had tasted Captain Hook
and it wanted more of him.

One day, Peter Pan and the children
went to the lake of mermaids.
They heard a loud cry for help
and they saw a big crocodile
chasing a little girl called Lily.
She was the daughter of the Indian chief.

Peter swooped down, grabbed Lily,
and flew her to safety.
"Thank you, Peter," Lily said.
"I was thrown to that crocodile
by cruel Captain Hook."

Peter Pan took Lily and the children
to the Indian village.

The Indian chief held a big feast
for Peter because he had saved his daughter.
The children danced with the Indians,
but Wendy was feeling sad.
She missed her mother and father.
It was time for her and her brothers
to go back home.

Wendy made her last meal
for the children of Neverland.
She baked a cake for Peter
and wrote him a goodbye note.

At that moment, the door burst open
and in rushed the pirates.
They tied up Wendy and her brothers,
and took them away to their ship.
Wicked Captain Hook put poison
in the cake made for Peter Pan.

Tinker Bell was hiding in the shadows
and she saw what had happened.
She saw Peter Pan come in.
"Where is everyone?" he said,
looking around the room.
Then he saw all the food.
"Wendy has made me a cake,"
he said. "It looks delicious!"

"No, no!" Tinker Bell flew to him
and snatched the cake away.
"Peter, don't eat that cake!
There's poison in it!"

"Tinker Bell, you are a liar,"
said Peter Pan.

Tinker Bell was sad. She said to Peter Pan,
"You do not believe me, so I will show you."
Then she took a bite of the poisoned cake.

She told him how Captain Hook's men
had taken Wendy and the boys.
"You'd better hurry," she said,
and she fell down, as pale as death.

"Tinker Bell!" he cried. "I'm so sorry!"
He put Tinker Bell on his lap
and wept tears over her.
The fairy opened her eyes.
"Peter, your loving heart has saved me.
Now you must save the children."

The children, tied with ropes, were on the ship.
In the sea were large hungry crocodiles
with their mouths wide open.

"Throw Wendy in first!" shouted Captain Hook.

The pirates pushed Wendy off the ship.
As she fell, Peter Pan swooped down
and grabbed her.

Peter Pan drew his sword.
"Captain Hook, I will fight you!"

"Ha ha!" cried Captain Hook.
"I've been waiting for this moment!"

Peter's sword smashed against the hook
and sparks flew. Clang! Clang!
While Peter Pan and Captain Hook
fought each other,
the brave children battled the pirates.
One by one, the pirates fell into the sea.

Captain Hook also lost his balance
and as he went over the side of the ship,
he heard a terrible sound below him.
Tick tock! Tick Tock! Tick tock!
"The crocodile!" he yelled
as he fell into its open mouth.

The children were very happy
that the pirates had gone,
but Wendy knew it was time to go.
Tinker Bell sprinkled her silver dust
and the ship rose up in the air.
Peter Pan steered it through the sky
until Wendy and her brothers were home.

"Come and live with us," said Wendy.

"No," said Peter Pan. "I must go back.
I want to live in Neverland forever."

Wendy and the boys watched
the pirate ship fly away
and disappear into the night.
They never saw Peter Pan again
but they never forgot him.